Mayor Hubble Is in Trouble!

Dan Gutman

Pictures by
Jim Paillot

HARPER
An Imprint of HarperCollinsPublishers

To Emma

My Weirder School #6: Mayor Hubble Is in Trouble!
Text copyright © 2012 by Dan Gutman
Illustrations copyright © 2012 by Jim Paillot
All rights reserved. Printed in the United States of America.
No part of this book may be used or reproduced in any manner whatsoever without written permission except in the case of brief quotations embodied in critical articles and reviews. For information address HarperCollins Children's Books, a division of HarperCollins Publishers, 195 Broadway, New York, NY 10007.
www.harpercollinschildrens.com
Library of Congress Cataloging-in-Publication Data is available.
ISBN 978-0-06-204213-2 (lib. bdg.) — ISBN 978-0-06-204212-5 (pbk.)
Typography by Kate Engbring
14 15 16   CG/RRDC   10 9 8 7 6 5 4 3
❖
First Edition

Contents

The Return of Mr. Wiggles

My name is A.J. and I hate ferrets.

Did you ever see a ferret? They are these disgusting brown animals that look like long, skinny rats.

My friend Neil, who we call the nude kid even though he wears clothes, has a pet ferret. His name is Mr. Wiggles. Last year Neil brought Mr. Wiggles to school on Crazy Pet Day. He escaped from his cage and climbed into a hat that belonged to this crybaby girl named Emily—while it was on her *head*! Emily freaked and went running out of the room.

It was hilarious. You should have been there! We saw it live and in person.

This year we didn't have Crazy Pet Day. We had Adopt-A-Pet Month. My teacher, Mr. Granite, said we could bring in a pet, and each of us would have to take it home for a night to take care of it.

"Okay, who brought in a furry friend today?" asked Mr. Granite, who is from another planet.

"I forgot," I said.

"I forgot," said my friend Ryan, who will eat anything, even stuff that isn't food.

"I forgot," said Michael, who never ties his shoes.

"I forgot," said Alexia, who is a girl that rides a skateboard all the time.

In case you were wondering, everybody was saying they forgot to bring in a pet. Except for one person.

Neil the nude kid.

"I remembered!" shouted Neil.

He took Mr. Wiggles out of his cage. Ugh. It was disgusting.

"He's adorable!" said all the girls.

"Kill him!" yelled all the boys except for Neil.

"I'm scared," said Emily, who's scared of everything.

"What can you tell us about your ferret, Neil?" asked Mr. Granite.

"Well, when Mr. Wiggles gets excited, he starts hopping sideways and bumping into things," Neil said. "It's called the weasel war dance."

"That's interesting!" said Mr. Granite. "Does anyone else know anything about ferrets?"

"*Ooooooooooooh! Ooooooooooooh!*" said Andrea Young, this girl with curly brown hair. She was waving her arm around like she was trying to be rescued from a desert island. Andrea is so annoying. In her spare

time, she reads the encyclopedia for fun.

"Male ferrets are called hobs," Andrea said, "and females are called jills."

"Very good, Andrea!" said Mr. Granite.

Why can't a truck full of ferrets fall on Andrea's head?

"What do ferrets eat?" asked Emily.

"They eat girls named Emily," I said.

"EEEEEEEEEEK!" Emily screamed, and then she went running out of the room.

Sheesh, get a grip! That girl will fall for anything.

Emily is weird. So are ferrets.*

---

* What does any of this have to do with Mayor Hubble?

The Shut-up Peace Sign

Neil put Mr. Wiggles in his cubby, and then we pledged the allegiance.

"Okay, let's get to work, shall we?" said Mr. Granite. "We're way behind and have a lot to cover. So turn to page twenty-three in your math book and—"

Mr. Granite didn't get the chance to finish

his sentence because an announcement came over the loudspeaker.

"All classes please report to the all-purpose room."

"Not *again*!" said Mr. Granite, slamming his math book shut.

We had to walk a million hundred miles to the all-purpose room, which is a room that is used for all purposes, so it has the perfect name. There were flags, banners, and red, white, and blue stuff all over the place. Nobody knew why. I had to sit next to Andrea. Ugh, disgusting!

Everybody was talking, so our principal, Mr. Klutz, made a peace sign with his fingers. That means "shut up." Everybody stopped talking.

"Election Day is coming up," said Mr. Klutz, who has no hair at all. "To help you learn about democracy, we're going to have elections at Ella Mentry School! Each of you will get to vote for one of your classmates to be president of your grade.

Doesn't that sound like fun?"

"Yes!" shouted all the girls.

"No!" shouted all the boys.

Then Mr. Klutz told us about democracy.

"In a democracy," he said, "all people have an equal say blah blah blah blah equality and freedom blah blah blah blah liberty blah blah blah blah Constitution blah blah blah blah majority rule blah blah blah blah the right to vote blah blah blah blah freedom of speech blah blah blah blah and whoever gets the most votes is the winner."

While Mr. Klutz was talking, kids started making faces, doodling in their notebooks, and shooting rubber bands at each other. I thought I was gonna die from old age.

But you'll never believe who came running into the door while Mr. Klutz was talking.

Nobody! It would hurt if you ran into a door! But you'll never believe who came running into the *doorway*.

It was Mayor Hubble!

"I thought Mayor Hubble was in jail," whispered Andrea.

He *was*. What happened was that gold had been discovered in our playground, and Mayor Hubble tried to steal it. But he was caught and sent to prison. We were all surprised to see him. He came

bounding up onto the stage followed by three bodyguards. They were big guys with necks that were almost as thick as their heads.

"Mayor Hubble!" said Mr. Klutz. "To what do we owe the pleasure of your company?* I thought you were in jail."

"I got time off for good behavior," Mayor Hubble said. "So I'm running for mayor again. I hope all the parents of your students will vote for me."

He made peace signs with both hands and waved them in the air while everybody clapped.

"Why is Mayor Hubble making the

* That's grown-up talk for "What are *you* doing here?"

shut-up peace sign?" I asked.

"That's not the shut-up peace sign, Arlo!" Andrea said, rolling her eyes. She calls me by my real name because she knows I don't like it. "He's making the V-for-Victory sign."

It looked just like the shut-up peace sign. If you ask me, they should have three different signs for "peace," "victory," and "shut up." It would be a lot less confusing.

I made a peace sign and stuck it in Andrea's face. But it didn't mean "peace" and it didn't mean "victory."

Rule the School

Later, we were having lunch in the vomitorium. That's a room that used to be called the cafetorium until some first grader threw up in there last year. Andrea and her girlie girl friends were sitting at the table next to us. Me and the guys let Alexia sit at our table because she's cool.

"Guess what?" Andrea said really loudly, so everybody would have to hear. "I decided that I'm going to run for president of the third grade!"

All the girls were hugging her and telling Andrea that she would make a great president.

"After I win the election," Andrea said, "I was thinking that we should have a dress code at Ella Mentry School. If we all wore uniforms, it would be easier to pick out our clothes in the morning."

"That's a great idea!" said Emily, who thinks all of Andrea's ideas are great.

"I really think we can make this school a better place," said Andrea.

"Hey, if you want to make the school a better place," I yelled to her, "why don't you switch to another school?"

"Oh, snap!" said Ryan.

"That's mean, Arlo!"

After lunch we went outside for recess. The guys and Alexia pulled me over to the corner by the monkey bars, where Andrea and her girlie girl friends couldn't hear us.

"The president rules the school, y'know," said Michael. "I don't want Andrea being in charge."

"I don't want to wear a uniform," said Alexia.

"Andrea will probably turn the school into a prison," said Ryan.

"It's gonna be horrible," said Neil the nude kid. "We need somebody to run against Andrea."

"Yeah," everybody agreed.

I looked around. Michael was looking at me. Ryan was looking at me. Alexia was looking at me. Neil was looking at me. *Everybody* was looking at me!

"What are you looking at me for?" I asked.

"You should run for president of the third grade, A.J.," said Alexia.

"Yeah!" everybody agreed.

"Why?" I asked. "I don't want to be president. That's for nerds."

"A.J., if you don't run, Andrea will become president," said Michael. "She's going to make us wear uniforms and turn the school into a prison."

"She'll probably close the boys' bathroom

and make us hold it in all day," said Ryan.

"So why don't one of *you* guys run?" I asked.

"You're the only one who can beat her,

A.J.," said Neil the nude kid.

"Well, I don't want to run," I said.

"A.J.," said Michael, "if you don't want to run against Andrea, that means you must be in love with her."

"That's right," everybody agreed.

"What?" I shouted. "It does not! It just means I don't want to be president."

"Oooooh!" Ryan said. "A.J. doesn't want to run against Andrea. They must be in *love!"*

"When are you and Andrea gonna get married?" asked Michael.

"Shhhhhhhhhh!" I said. "Okay! Okay! I'll run for president of the third grade."

If those guys weren't my best friends, I would hate them.

Super Secret Strategy Session

We needed to have a meeting in a place where Andrea and her girlie girl friends couldn't spy on us. Ryan has a cool tree house in his backyard, so we decided to meet up there. Michael, Neil, and Alexia came over to Ryan's house after school.

"I don't know anything about elections,"

I told the gang. "How am I going to beat Andrea? Does anybody have any ideas?"

"You need a slogan," suggested Alexia. "Like, 'A.J. Puts the *Cool* in School.'"

"You should get the No Bell Prize for that," I said.*

"How about, 'A.J. Puts the *Drool* in School'?" suggested Michael.

"That doesn't make any sense," said Ryan. "There's no *d-r* in the word 'school.'"

"We should make a commercial and put it on TV during the Super Bowl," suggested Neil the nude kid.

"The Super Bowl is in January," said

---

* That's a prize they give out to people who don't have bells.

Michael. "It's too late. The election is in November."

"How about we make one of those Batman signs and project it on the sky at night?" suggested Ryan.

"That's dumb," I told him.

"Hey, nobody likes to floss, right?" said Alexia. "So what if we knock on people's doors, show them how to floss correctly, and tell them to vote for A.J.?"

"That's the dumbest idea in the history of the world," said Neil the nude kid.

"Well, I'm stumped," said Michael.

"Your legs were amputated?" I asked.

"No, dumbhead," he replied. "Stumped means—"

But he didn't get the chance to finish his sentence. You'll never believe in a million hundred years whose head popped up into the tree house at that moment.

It was Mayor Hubble!

"I heard you were running for president of the third grade, A.J.," he told me. "I came to help you win the election."

"How did you know we would be holding our supersecret strategy session up *here*?" asked Ryan.

"I was a boy once, you know," said the mayor.

"Just once?" I said. "I'm a boy *all* the time."

"Look, A.J." said the mayor. "Let's get

down to business. You don't like Andrea,
do you?"

"No!"

"You want to *beat* her on Election Day,
don't you?"

"Yeah!"

"You want to *humiliate* her, right?"

"Yeah!!"

"You want her to wish she was never born!"

"YEAH!!!"

"Well, I have a plan to help you win the election," said the mayor.

"What is it?" we all asked.

"I'm not going to tell you," said the mayor.

"Why not?" asked Neil.

"Okay, okay, I'll tell you," the mayor said. "But you have to wait until the next chapter."

"Why can't you tell us in *this* chapter?" asked Ryan.

"Because this chapter is almost over," said Mayor Hubble. "There's no room."

"Why don't you just make this chapter a little longer," asked Michael, "and tell us *now*?"

"Wait a minute," Alexia said. "Why are you guys talking about chapters? Are we in a book or something?"

"Of *course* we're in a book," I told Alexia. "It's a series called My Weirder School."

"Never heard of it," Alexia said.

"That's because you're new," I told her.

"It doesn't matter," said Mayor Hubble. "A.J., the point is that if you do what I tell you to do, you'll beat Andrea in the election."

"Why do *you* care whether or not I win the election?" I asked.

"Because if I help you beat Andrea," said the mayor, "maybe you can do something for *me*. You scratch my back, and I'll scratch yours."

"What does back scratching have to do with anything?" I asked. "My back doesn't even itch."

"A.J.," said the mayor, "after I help you win the election, the only thing you need to do is tell all the parents to vote for me.

Can you do that?"

I looked at Ryan. Ryan looked at Neil. Neil looked at Michael. Michael looked at Alexia. Alexia looked at me.

"It's a deal," I said.

"Great," said the mayor. "Let's keep this our little secret."

"My lips are sealed," I said.

But not with glue or anything. That would be weird.

Yuck!
Kissing! Gross!

When I got to school the next day, kids and parents were sitting all over the front steps. There were posters, banners, and signs hanging on the fence.

VOTE FOR ANDREA:
Gifted, Talented, and Ready!

A.J. PUTS THE COOL IN SCHOOL!

Ryan, Michael, and Neil the nude kid were standing around in black T-shirts with their arms crossed in front of them and scowls on their faces.

"What's up with you guys?" I asked.

"We're your bodyguards," Ryan told me. "We have to look mean."

"Yeah," said Neil the nude kid. "Somebody might try to attack you."

"If somebody messes with you, we'll take care of them," said Michael, punching a fist into his open hand.

"Who told you to dress like that?" I asked them. "And who made all these signs?"

They all looked over at the sidewalk, where Mayor Hubble was leaning against a telephone pole. He winked at me, and I went over to him.

Andrea was up at the top of the steps, standing at a podium.

". . . so in conclusion," Andrea said, "that's why you should vote for *me* to be the president of the third grade. Thank you."

The kids sitting on the steps clapped and cheered and waved little flags for Little Miss Perfect.

"Great job, Andrea!" said Mr. Klutz. "Now it's time to hear from the *other* candidate for third-grade president . . . A.J.!"

What?! I didn't know what to say. I didn't know what to do. I had to think fast.

"Nobody told me I had to give a speech," I whispered to Mayor Hubble.

"Don't worry about it," he said, slipping me a sheet of paper. "Just read this."

"What is it?"

"It's your stump speech."

"You want me to speak to people with no legs?" I asked.

"Not *that* kind of stump," the mayor said. "A stump speech is a standard political speech that you give over and over again."

I climbed the steps and stood behind the podium. Everybody was clapping and cheering like crazy.

I was nervous! I had never given a speech before. I started to read from the piece of paper Mayor Hubble gave me.

"Four score and seven years ago," I said, "I had a dream. I had a dream that the ballot was stronger than the bullet. The pen was mightier than the sword. And those who stand for nothing fall for anything. Now, fellow students, I've been to the mountaintop, and I can tell you this. Ask not what your school can do for you; ask what *you* can do for your school. The only thing we have to fear is fear itself. Give me liberty or give me death! Read my lips! Tear down this wall! The time for change has come! No man is an island. But if you vote for me, life, liberty, and the pursuit of happiness shall not perish from this earth. Thank you."

Everybody was going crazy. Alexia was the first one to congratulate me.

"That was terrific, A.J.!"

"What did I just say?" I asked her.

"Who cares?" she replied. "Listen to that applause!"

On the other side of the steps, I saw that Andrea was going around shaking hands

with everybody. So I figured I had to do that too. My bodyguards surrounded me as I walked around shaking hands with people on the sidewalk. That's when the weirdest thing in the history of the world happened.

Some lady stuck a baby in my face!

"Ahhhhhhhhh!" I screamed. "What is this baby doing here? It's too young to be in school."

"Never mind that, A.J.," Alexia whispered. "Kiss the baby."

"I'm not kissing a baby!" I replied. "I don't even like kissing my *mother* when people are around."

"Kissing babies is part of running for

office, A.J.," said Michael. "You *have* to do it."

"Why?" I asked. "Babies can't vote."

"You don't want to kiss my baby?" asked the lady. She looked all sad.

"A.J., it will look bad if you don't kiss the baby," said Ryan. "You're going to lose the election, and Andrea will be president."

"And if you don't kiss the baby," said Neil, "that means you love Andrea."

"I do not!" I protested.

"Kiss it, A.J.," said Alexia.

I looked at the baby. The baby looked at me. It was drooling. I didn't know what to say. I didn't know what to do. I wished I could just run away to Antarctica and live with the penguins.

I kissed the baby.

And when I leaned over to kiss the baby, I'm pretty sure I smelled something. Something bad.

"I think the baby pooped!" I yelled.

Ugh, disgusting! I thought I was gonna die.

On the Stump

Later that day, Mayor Hubble showed up in the playground at recess. Man, ever since he got out of jail, that guy sure has a lot of time on his hands! The gang and me were playing on the monkey bars when the mayor came over.

"It's time to go on the stump, A.J."

"Do you want me to stand on a tree that was cut down?"

"Not *that* kind of stump," Mayor Hubble said.* "I mean you've got to campaign for votes."

Andrea was standing on the top of the swing set nearby. A bunch of kids were gathered on the ground listening to her talk.

"When I'm president of the third grade," Andrea said, "I promise there will be plenty of pencils and paper and glue sticks and scissors and crayons in every class. Ella

---

* Okay, okay, I promise there won't be any more stump jokes.

43

Mentry School will be the best school in the state!"

"Yay!" Everybody was cheering.

The gang turned to look at me.

"What are *you* going to promise to do when *you're* president, A.J.?" asked Mayor Hubble.

"How should I know?"

"Andrea is making all kinds of promises," said Ryan, "so you've got to make some promises too if you want to win."

"What kind of promises?" I asked.

"It doesn't matter," said Mayor Hubble. "As long as you get the kids to vote for you."

I climbed up on the top of the monkey bars.

"Attention, third graders!" I shouted. "I have an important announcement."

All the kids who were listening to Andrea came over to the monkey bars.

"When I'm president of the third grade," I shouted, "I promise there will be no more homework!"

"Yay!" Everybody started chanting, "No more homework!"

Andrea had on her mean face.

"I have an important announcement," she shouted. Some of the kids went back over to her. "When I'm president, we will have fewer fire drills. That way we'll be able to spend more time learning."

"Yay!"

"Can you possibly be any more boring?"

I shouted to Andrea. "When I'm president, we'll have *more* fire drills! In fact, we'll have a fire drill *every* day! With *real* fires!"

"Yay!"

Andrea looked madder than ever. The kids didn't know if they should listen to her or me, so they started running back and forth between us.

"When I'm president," Andrea shouted, "every student in the school will get their own iPad! You won't have to carry a heavy backpack anymore, because all your books will be on the iPad!"

"Yay!"

"When I'm president," I shouted, "there will be a video game system built into every desk in the school!"

"Yay!"

"When I'm president," Andrea shouted, "the water fountains will be filled with lemonade!"

"Yay!"

"When I'm president," I shouted, "every day will be a snow day, even if there's no snow! And we're going to have *rain* days too! After all, rain is just extremely wet snow."

"Yay!"

"And furthermore," I shouted, "we're going to take all the hard words out of the dictionary. And we're going to abolish anything higher than the five times table. Kids will no longer have to sit in the corner when they misbehave. We're going to make all the classrooms round, so there will be no corners! And all the teachers will be fired and replaced by comic book superheroes!"

"Yay!"

"Top *that,* Andrea!" I shouted. "In your face!"

Andrea was really mad! It looked like she couldn't think of anything else to promise.

"If you vote for *me,*" she finally shouted, "I'll give each of you ... a dollar!"

"Gasp!" everybody gasped. Then they started cheering.

"Yay!"

"If you vote for *me,*" I shouted, "I'll give

you *two* dollars!"

"Yay!"

"I'll give you *three* dollars, and a candy bar!" shouted Andrea.

"Yay!"

We went back and forth like that for a while. Making promises is fun!

How to Wash a Ferret

The next day was the worst day in the history of the world. It was my turn to bring home Mr. Wiggles—Neil the nude kid's disgusting pet ferret.

"Have fun with Mr. Wiggles," Mr. Granite said when the bell rang.

"Have fun with Mr. Wiggles," said Ryan.

"Have fun with Mr. Wiggles," said Emily.

In case you were wondering, everybody was telling me to have fun with Mr. Wiggles. The only one who didn't say that was Neil, who told me to be sure to take care of Mr. Wiggles. He gave me some ferret food.

Ferrets are gross. I had to carry the cage home from school with me.

"He's adorable!" said my older sister, Amy. "Can I hold him?"

"Just be careful," I told her. "If Mr. Wiggles escapes, I'm in big trouble."

Amy picked up Mr. Wiggles and was rocking him in her arms like he was a baby. He didn't like it, and he started trying to hop back and forth.

"He's doing the weasel war dance," I told her. "That means he's excited. You'd better stop playing with him."

Amy put Mr. Wiggles back in his cage.

"How do you wash a ferret?" Amy asked.

"I guess you put it in a washing machine," I said. "Then you dry it in a microwave oven."

"You do not, A.J.!"

My mom forced me to keep Mr. Wiggles in my bedroom all night. It was creepy. He just sat in his cage and stared at me.

I closed my eyes for a while, and when I opened them again, Mr. Wiggles was still staring at me with those beady little ferret

eyes. It was hard to sleep.

"I like penguins," I whispered to Mr. Wiggles. "Do you have any penguin friends?"

Mr. Wiggles didn't answer. He just stared at me.

"Penguins are cool," I told him. "I wish you were a penguin. You would be my best friend."

Mr. Wiggles just sat there and stared at me some more. He was boring.

I decided that when I'm president of the third grade, the first thing I'll do is cancel Adopt-A-Pet Month. And I will ban ferrets from Ella Mentry School forever.

"You are ugly," I whispered to Mr. Wiggles.

Mr. Wiggles just stared at me.

"You are a dumbhead," I said.

Mr. Wiggles stared at me some more.

He doesn't even understand English.

"When I count to three, sit there and do nothing," I said. "One . . . two . . . three."

Mr. Wiggles just stared at me. Wow, that was amazing! I had taught him a trick!

Mr. Wiggles wasn't that much fun to be around, but I had a good time insulting a ferret.

The Great Debate

I was walking with Mr. Wiggles to school the next morning when a big, black limo pulled up alongside me. The window rolled down. Mayor Hubble was inside.

"Hop in, A.J.," he said. "I'll give you a ride."

I had never been in a limo before. I got

in, putting Mr. Wiggles's cage on the seat between us.

"What's that?" the mayor asked.

"A ferret."

"It looks like a long rat," said the mayor. "A.J., I wanted to tell you that you're doing great. There's no way Andrea can win the election. But you still need to debate with her."

"I need to go fishing with Andrea?" I asked.

"Not 'the bait'!" said the mayor. "'*De*bate'!"

I was just yanking the mayor's chain. I know what a debate is. That's when two people shake hands, and then they argue for a while, and then they shake hands again and pretend they weren't arguing.

Mayor Hubble told me the big debate would be that afternoon. He said he wouldn't be there because he didn't want anybody to know he was helping me win the election. The limo stopped a block from the school to let me out.

"Remember our deal," Mayor Hubble

said. "After you win, you tell all the parents to vote for me."

"Got it," I said.

I was nervous all morning. I couldn't look at Andrea. Mr. Granite taught us some stuff about social studies, but I wasn't paying attention. All I could think about was the big debate.

Finally, it was two o'clock. We had to go to the all-purpose room. The whole third grade was there. Up on the stage were two podiums. I climbed up the steps and stood behind one of them. Andrea went and stood behind the other one. Our librarian, Mrs. Roopy, stood between us.

"Good afternoon, third graders," she

said. "Welcome to the great debate. Isn't this exciting?"

"Yes!" shouted all the girls.

"No!" shouted all the boys.

"We're going to keep this pretty simple," said Mrs. Roopy. "I will ask questions, and each candidate will give a brief answer. Ready? Let's start with you, Andrea. Why do you want to be president of the third grade?"

"That's an excellent question, Mrs. Roopy," said Andrea, who is a big brownnoser. "I want to be president of the third grade so I can help improve the quality of our education here at Ella Mentry School and blah blah blah blah

blah . . ."

Andrea went on and on for a million hundred hours. I thought I was gonna die.

"And why do *you* want to be president,

A.J.?" asked Mrs. Roopy.

"I want to be president so Andrea will not win," I admitted. "Because if she's president, we'll all be marching around in uniforms, doing extra homework, reading Shakespeare plays, taking dancing lessons, and singing songs from *Annie*."

"That's a lie!" Andrea protested.

"Let's move on," said Mrs. Roopy. "What do you think should be served for lunch at our cafetorium? Andrea?"

"I believe the students should have a healthy, nutritious meal every day," Andrea said. "And I will fight so that each and every one of us gets a balanced diet."

"That's right!" shouted Emily.

"I think we should be able to eat as much junk food as we want," I said.

"So, Andrea," said Mrs. Roopy, "would you ban junk food from the cafetorium?"

"Yes!" Andrea replied. "How will we grow up to be big and strong if we stuff ourselves with that poison?"

"There you go again," I said. "You want to take away our freedom, the freedom to poison ourselves. That's in the Bill of Rights, y'know."

"It is not!" Andrea shouted. "I memorized the Bill of Rights, and that's not one of them!"

"*My* Bill of Rights came with bonus features," I said. "Like a DVD."

Everybody laughed, even though I didn't say anything funny.

"Let's move on," said Mrs. Roopy. "Andrea, you have said that recess is too long and that it takes time away from learning. But most kids say that recess is too short. What is your feeling now?"

"Well, I was for recess before I was against recess," Andrea said.

"Make up your mind!" I shouted at Andrea. "You're a flip-flopper!"

"I am not!" Andrea shouted. "You're mean, Arlo!"

"So is your face!" I replied.

"Well, you're not invited to my birthday party!" Andrea shouted at me.

Everybody gasped. Not inviting a kid to your birthday party is just about the meanest thing you can do to somebody.

"I don't want to go to your dumb birthday party *anyway*!" I shouted back at her.

"Okay, settle down, everyone," said Mrs. Roopy. "Describe for me the perfect class field trip. You first, A.J."

"We would go see the new Batman movie before it comes out," I said. "Free popcorn for everybody. That would be cool!"

"Andrea?"

"We would fly to Paris and visit the Louvre museum," said Andrea. "We would see the *Mona Lisa* and all the wonderful works of art there."

We went back and forth like that for a while. Whenever I said anything, kids would clap and cheer. Whenever Little Miss I-Know-Everything said anything, the only one who clapped or cheered was Emily. I was definitely winning the debate.

"It's time for the closing arguments," said Mrs. Roopy. "Each candidate will have five minutes to say whatever they want. Andrea, you may go first."

"I would just like to say that blah blah blah blah blah and that's why you should vote for me."

"Okay, A.J., you have the floor."

"Why would I want a floor?" I asked.

"That means it's your turn to talk, dumbhead!" yelled Andrea, rolling her eyes.

"I knew that," I lied. "Well, my opponent has spent the last million hundred minutes spreading nasty lies and calling me names," I said. "So I would like to conclude by saying that ANDREA IS A POOPY HEAD! That's why you should vote for me. Thank you!"

The kids went crazy. All you have to do is say the words "poopy head" and kids go crazy. Nobody knows why.

The great debate was over. I had totally mopped the floor with Andrea.* It was the greatest day of my life.

---

* But not really. You should mop the floor with a *mop*. Mopping the floor with a person is weird.

Playing Hardball

There were only two days before the election, and things were looking good. Just about all the kids in third grade said they were going to vote for me. Hardly anybody wanted Andrea to be president. Nobody wanted to wear a uniform and give up recess. Except for Emily, of course.

"You're a shoo-in, A.J.," Michael told me.

I had no idea what shoes had to do with anything.

That's when the worst thing in the history of the world happened. When I got to school the next day, everybody was holding a sheet of pink paper. I picked one up off the ground. This is what it said. . . .

THINGS YOU DON'T KNOW
ABOUT A.J. . . .

- He throws paper into the garbage instead of putting it in the recycling box!

- He changed a C– to a C+ on his spelling test last week!

- He wears the same underwear two days in a row!

- He didn't get his mother a card for Mother's Day!

- He uses a magnifying glass to torture defenseless insects!

- He picks his nose and eats it!

♥ VOTE FOR ANDREA: ♥
Gifted, Talented, and Ready!

Those were lies!

Well, most of them were anyway.

All the kids were talking to each other. I heard some of them saying that they were thinking of voting for Andrea instead of me.

This was the worst thing to happen since TV Turnoff Week! I called for an emergency strategy session, and the gang gathered in Ryan's tree house as soon as school let out that day.

"Did you *really* forget to make your mom a card for Mother's Day, A.J.?" asked Alexia.

"I didn't forget!" I said. "I ran out of time."

"That's just *wrong*, man," said Michael.

"Gee, maybe I should vote for Andrea,"

said Neil the nude kid. "I'm not sure I could vote for a kid who doesn't make his mom a Mother's Day card."

"I might vote for Andrea too," said Ryan.

"You *can't* vote for Andrea!" I shouted at them. "You're the ones who talked me into this in the first place! I didn't want to run for president!"

That's when the weirdest thing in the history of the world happened. Mayor Hubble popped his head up into the tree house.

"I saw that flyer that Andrea printed up," the mayor said. "That girl is very tricky. A.J., it's time for us to play hardball."

"I didn't bring my glove," I told him.

"Not *that* kind of hardball!" said the mayor. "We need to dig up some dirt."

"Should I get a shovel?" I asked.

"Not *that* kind of dirt! Andrea dug up dirt about you. So you need to dig up some dirt about Andrea. It's the only way you can win the election."

"How can we dig up dirt about Andrea?" asked Alexia.

"Follow me," said the mayor.

We all piled into Mayor Hubble's limo and drove over to Andrea's house. The

limo driver parked a block away, across the street.

"What are we doing *here*?" I asked. "Andrea's never home after school. She's always taking some dance class or piano lesson so she'll be better than everybody else."

"I know," Mayor Hubble whispered. "That's why we're going to her house *now*."

Mayor Hubble sneaked down the street, hiding behind trees and bushes like he was a secret agent. We all followed him.

"What if Andrea's parents are home?" asked Alexia.

"*Shhhhhhhhhh!*" Mayor Hubble said. "Her parents are at work."

"I don't feel good about this," said Ryan.

Mayor Hubble led us to the back door of Andrea's house. He searched around until he found a key under the welcome mat.

"Aha!" he said as he put the key into the lock.

"Isn't it illegal to break into somebody's house?" I asked.

"I'm not breaking in," said the mayor. "I'm using the key."

"I can't do this," Neil said. "It's wrong."

"*You're* not doing it," Mayor Hubble said.

"I'm doing it. And I'm the former mayor, so it's okay."

He turned the key and pushed open the door. I was afraid an alarm would go off, but it didn't.

"Follow me," the mayor said. "Let's go upstairs to Andrea's room."

We slinked up the stairs like secret agents.

"What if we get caught?" whispered Michael.

"Shhhhhhhhhhhh!" said Mayor Hubble.

It wasn't hard to find Andrea's room. It was the one with all the pink in it.

"WOW!" everybody said, which is "MOM" upside down.

The walls were pink. The bedspread was pink. The rug was pink. The stuffed animals, dolls, and other girlie girl stuff all over the place were pink. I thought I was gonna go blind from all the pinkness.

"Andrea sure wins a lot of awards," said Alexia.

There was a bookcase filled with trophies, plaques, ribbons, and certificates with Andrea's name all over everything.

"We should get out of here," I said. "She might come home any second."

"Shhhhhhh!" said Mayor Hubble. "Look what I found!"

He was holding a book that was on the desk. The cover said ANDREA'S PRIVATE DIARY.

"I'll bet there's some good dirt in here," Mayor Hubble said.

"You can't read that!" said Michael.

"Sure I can," said the mayor. "I'm the former mayor."

He flipped through the pages. We all gathered around so we could look over his shoulder.

Most of the pages were just boring stuff about Andrea's dance class, Andrea's gymnastics class, Andrea's art class. . . .

And then the mayor turned to a page with just three words on it. Three *horrible* words. The worst words in the history of the world . . .

I LIKE A.J.!

Ahhhhhhhhhhhhh!

"Oooooh!" Ryan said. "Andrea likes A.J. They must be in *love!*"

"When are you and Andrea gonna get married?" asked Michael.

"Can we get out of here now?" I asked.

I wanted to run away to Antarctica and live with the penguins.

Signs of Trouble

I didn't want to go to school the next day. I didn't want to go to school for the rest of my life. Once word got around that Andrea wrote "I LIKE A.J." in her diary, my life would be over anyway.

So I walked *really* slowly to school. If you walk slowly enough to someplace you don't want to go, you'll never get there. That's the first rule of being a kid.

A big, black limo pulled up next to me.

"Psssssssst!" said Mayor Hubble as he rolled down the window. "Hop in!"

As we rode to school, he pointed to all the yard signs that people had put up on their front lawns: VOTE FOR ANDREA. VOTE FOR A.J.

"I have a job for you," the mayor told me. "You need to take down all the Vote for Andrea signs and replace them with Vote for Mayor Hubble signs."

"Isn't that stealing?" I asked.

"No, don't be silly," the mayor said, "it's *borrowing.* It's sort of like borrowing a book from the library. After the election you can give the signs back."

"I don't know," I said. "It seems kind of wrong to me."

"Look," said the mayor, "the election is tomorrow. I thought you said you wanted to beat Andrea."

"I do."

"I thought you wanted to *humiliate* her."

"I do!"

"I thought you wanted her to wish she had never been born."

"I *do*!!"

"Well, if you want to win the election, A.J., you need to take down Andrea's yard signs," said the mayor. "We didn't dig up any good dirt on her. This is the only way."

"Okay." I sighed. "If you say so."

"Good boy," said Mayor Hubble as he handed me a bunch of VOTE FOR MAYOR HUBBLE signs.

After dinner that night I told my parents I was going over to Ryan's house to check our homework. But I didn't go to Ryan's house. I grabbed the VOTE FOR MAYOR HUBBLE signs and went out looking for some VOTE FOR ANDREA signs.

It was getting dark outside. I was slinking around the neighborhood like a secret agent. It was cool. At the first house I came to, there were *two* signs on the front lawn. One said VOTE FOR ANDREA and the other said VOTE FOR A.J.

I started pulling the VOTE FOR ANDREA sign out of the ground. And you'll never believe in a million hundred guesses who tapped me on the shoulder at that moment.

It was Andrea!

"Ahhhhhhhhhhhh!" I shouted.

She was holding an armful of VOTE FOR MAYOR HUBBLE yard signs, just like I was.

"Arlo, what are *you* doing here?" she asked.

"I'm taking away your yard signs," I told her. "What are *you* doing here?"

"I came to take away *your* yard signs!" she said. "Who told you to do this?"

"Mayor Hubble," I told Andrea. "He told me to take down your signs and replace them with Vote for Mayor Hubble signs."

"That's strange," said Andrea. "He told me to take down *your* signs and replace them with Vote for Mayor Hubble signs *too*!"

Andrea and I looked at each other for a second.

"You mean Mayor Hubble is helping *you* win the election?" I asked Andrea.

"Yes!"

"Mayor Hubble has been helping *you* win the election *too*?" Andrea asked me.

"Yeah!" I said. "He told me he would help me win if I told all the parents to vote for him."

"That's the same thing he told *me*!" said Andrea. "So no matter which of us wins, it will be good for Mayor Hubble!"

She looked really mad.

"Mayor Hubble is in trouble," she said.

And the Winner Is . . .

Finally, it was Election Day. There was a ballot box for each grade in the front hallway so kids could vote before going to class.

"Good luck, man," said Michael.

"I hope you win," said Neil the nude kid.

"It's in the bag, A.J.," said Ryan.

"*What's* in the bag?" I asked. "You don't even have a bag."

After I voted (for myself, of course), I went to the boy's bathroom and put on a fake nose and glasses I brought from home. Then I went back to the table with the ballot boxes.

"My name is Bob," I said. "I'd like to vote in the third-grade election."

"Certainly," said the mom behind the ballot box.

After I voted (for myself again, of course), I went back to the boy's bathroom and put on the Batman costume that was in my backpack. Then I went back to the table.

"My name is Batman," I said. "I'd like to vote in the third-grade election."

"Thanks for voting!" said the mom as she handed me another ballot.

I must have voted for myself at least ten times. At that point I ran out of disguises and walked down the hall to class. That's when Andrea stopped me in the hallway.

"I just wanted to say good luck, Arlo," she said, "even though I hope you lose."

"I hope you lose too," I told Andrea. "So good luck losing."

I was about to walk away, but I stopped.

"Hey Andrea," I said, "can I ask you a question?"

"Sure, Arlo. What is it?"

"I just wanted to know," I said, looking at my feet, "do you like me?"

I knew I shouldn't have said it. As soon as the words left my mouth, I wanted to stuff them back inside. But it was too late.

Andrea didn't answer for like a million

hundred seconds. It was so quiet. It was like we were in an underground cave, and all the other humans had been eaten by zombies.

And then Andrea said those three little words.

"Of course not," she said. "I can't stand you."

"Well, I can't stand you either," I told her.

"Okay, then we're in agreement," Andrea said. "May the better candidate win."

I didn't say anything else to her as we walked down the hall to class.

After we pledged the allegiance and did Word of the Day, the whole third grade was called to the all-purpose room to find out who won the election.

When we got there, there was electricity in the air. Well, not really. If there was electricity in the air, we would all die.

I spotted Mayor Hubble sitting in the front row. He winked at me. Mr. Klutz climbed up on the stage and made the shut-up victory peace sign. Everybody stopped talking. He took a sheet of paper out of his pocket.

"I hope this election helped you kids learn how democracy works," Mr. Klutz told us. "You picked your candidates. You watched them campaign. You listened to them debate. You voted. And now the votes have been counted, and it's time to reveal the results. The president of the third grade is . . ."

I'm not gonna tell you.

Okay okay, I'll tell you. But you have to read the next chapter. So nah-nah-nah boo-boo on you!

The Runoff

Mr. Klutz was about to announce the winner of the election. We were all on pins and needles.

Well, not really. That would hurt.

"The president of the third grade is . . . NOBODY!"

"Gasp!" everybody gasped.

"Nobody?" I yelled.

"I'm sorry," said Mr. Klutz, "but A.J. and Andrea have both been disqualified."

"Why?" everybody was asking.

"I have been informed that Mayor Hubble was helping both of them," said Mr. Klutz. "Officer Spence, arrest that man!"

Our security guard, Officer Spence, came running over to Mayor Hubble.

"You're under arrest!" he said as he slapped a pair of handcuffs on the mayor.

"On what charge?" demanded Mayor Hubble.

"Trespassing, stealing yard signs, contributing to the delinquency of minors . . ."

"B-but . . . ," said Mayor Hubble.

Everybody started giggling because the mayor said "but," which sounds just like "butt" except it's missing a *t*.*

"That's not fair!" Mayor Hubble yelled as Officer Spence dragged him away. "I'm not a crook, I tell you! I'm an honest man! I want my lawyer!"

After Mr. Klutz made the shut-up victory peace sign and everybody calmed down, the teachers went around passing out slips of paper and pencils to all the kids.

"We're going to have a runoff election to determine the president of the third grade," Mr. Klutz told us. "You can vote for anyone you want, as long as it's not

---

*Grown-ups get mad when you say "butt." Nobody knows why.

A.J. or Andrea."

Andrea was upset that she was disqualified, but I didn't care. I didn't want to be president anyway. I just didn't want *her* to be president.

We all voted again, and the teachers collected the slips of paper. It took about a million hundred hours for them to count up all the votes. Finally, Mr. Klutz went back to the microphone.

"The winner of the runoff election, and the president of the third grade is . . . ," he said, ". . . Mr. Wiggles? Who's Mr. Wiggles?"

WHAT?!

Neil the nude kid's pet ferret was the president of the third grade? Everybody was hooting and hollering.

Neil was told to go get Mr. Wiggles. He went running to class and came back with Mr. Wiggles in his cage.

"Hooray for Mr. Wiggles!" we started chanting. "Hooray for Mr. Wiggles!"

Neil took Mr. Wiggles out of his cage and held him up in the air so we could all see him. Everybody went crazy. It was really loud.

"Hooray for Mr. Wiggles!"

That's when the weirdest thing in the history of the world happened. Mr. Wiggles must have been really excited about winning the election, because he started doing his weasel war dance and jumped out of Neil's hands!

And then, after winning the runoff election, Mr. Wiggles ran off! He hopped down from the stage and headed straight for the front row.

"EEEEEEEEEEEEEEEEEEK!" somebody shouted. "There's a wild ferret on the loose!"

"Help!"

"Run for your lives!"

Kids were screaming, yelling, crying, clawing each other, and knocking each other over to get out of the way. You should have been there.

All in all, it sure made for an exciting Election Day! Maybe Neil will find Mr. Wiggles. Maybe grown-ups will stop saying "Blah blah blah blah." Maybe Andrea will invite me to her birthday party. Maybe people will stop running into doors. Maybe we'll go on a field trip to see the new Batman movie. Maybe people will stop talking about stumps all the time. Maybe Alexia will realize she is a fictional character. Maybe ladies will stop sticking babies in my face. Maybe I'll make a Mother's Day card for my mom next year. Maybe the guys will stop saying I love Andrea. Maybe Mayor Hubble will find a way to get out of jail again.

But it won't be easy!